caillou®

Goes Camping

Adaptation of
the animated series:
Roger Harvey
Illustrations:
CINAR Animation

chouette CINAR

Caillou was playing hide-and-seek with Grandpa.
He tiptoed into the living room. "Where are you, Grandpa?"
He climbed up on the big chair and peeked behind it.
"Found you!" Caillou laughed.

Grandpa tried to get away, but Caillou jumped on his back and threw his arms around Grandpa's neck.

Just then, Daddy appeared in
the doorway.
"Come on, you two. Snack's ready.
We're waiting for you in the
backyard."
"Coming, Daddy!"
Caillou poked Grandpa gently
in the back. "Giddyup, horsey!"

Out in the yard, Mommy
had just set the table for
their snack. There were
cookies, cake, fruit, and
cold drinks on the table.
Grandpa arrived carrying
Caillou piggyback.

"This reminds me of the first time I took your daddy camping when he was a little boy, just like you," said Grandpa.

"You went camping with Daddy?" Caillou asked.

"We sure did!" replied Grandpa. "We even saw a raccoon and went swimming in a big lake."

That gave Caillou an idea. "Grandpa, why don't we go camping, just you and me?"

"A camping trip takes a lot of planning, Caillou," said his mommy, who was listening.
"It might not take too much work," replied Grandpa.

Now Grandpa had an idea! "Do you still have your old camping tent?" he asked Caillou's mommy.
She nodded.
"Well, then, I think I know just the spot to go camping," said Grandpa.

Caillou helped Grandpa set up the tent under the big tree in the backyard. He held one of the poles while Grandpa was busy inside the tent. Suddenly a squirrel darted across the lawn. Caillou dropped the pole and ran after the little animal.
The tent started to wobble dangerously. Grandpa called for help.
"Caillou? Caillou, what are you doing?"
Too late! The tent collapsed on top of Grandpa.
Caillou came back, looking sheepish.

"This time, Caillou, I'll hold the front and you go inside the tent."
Caillou crawled under the flap. Grandpa called out instructions.
"Keep going until you get to the pole."
"Where?" asked Caillou.
"Hmm," sighed Grandpa. "I'd better show you."

He joined Caillou in the tent.
But as soon as he
went inside, the
tent collapsed again.
Laughing, the two
campers struggled
to get out.

Suddenly, Caillou heard the sound of birds chirping.
"Look, Grandpa, a bird's nest!" he said, pointing to the tree.
Grandpa picked up Caillou and lifted him off the ground to see the bird feeding its young.
"Grandpa, there are two baby birds in the nest!" exclaimed Caillou.

Grandpa put Caillou back down. "We'd better get our tent up or we'll be spending the night under the stars."

Later that evening, Caillou and Grandpa sat cross-legged on the ground, roasting marshmallows over a small fire. Caillou pushed his stick near the flame. "Not too close, Caillou!" Grandpa warned. Caillou blew on his marshmallow to cool it down.
"They look perfect!" said Grandpa, popping one into his mouth.
"Mmm! Delicious!"

Caillou thought Grandpa looked funny with his bulging cheeks.
"You look like a big squirrel," he laughed.
Grandpa laughed too.
Caillou decided camping with Grandpa was lots of fun.

When it got dark, they wrapped themselves up in blankets and lay back admiring the starry sky. Grandpa started to yawn.
"It's getting late. I'll get our sleeping bags ready," he said.

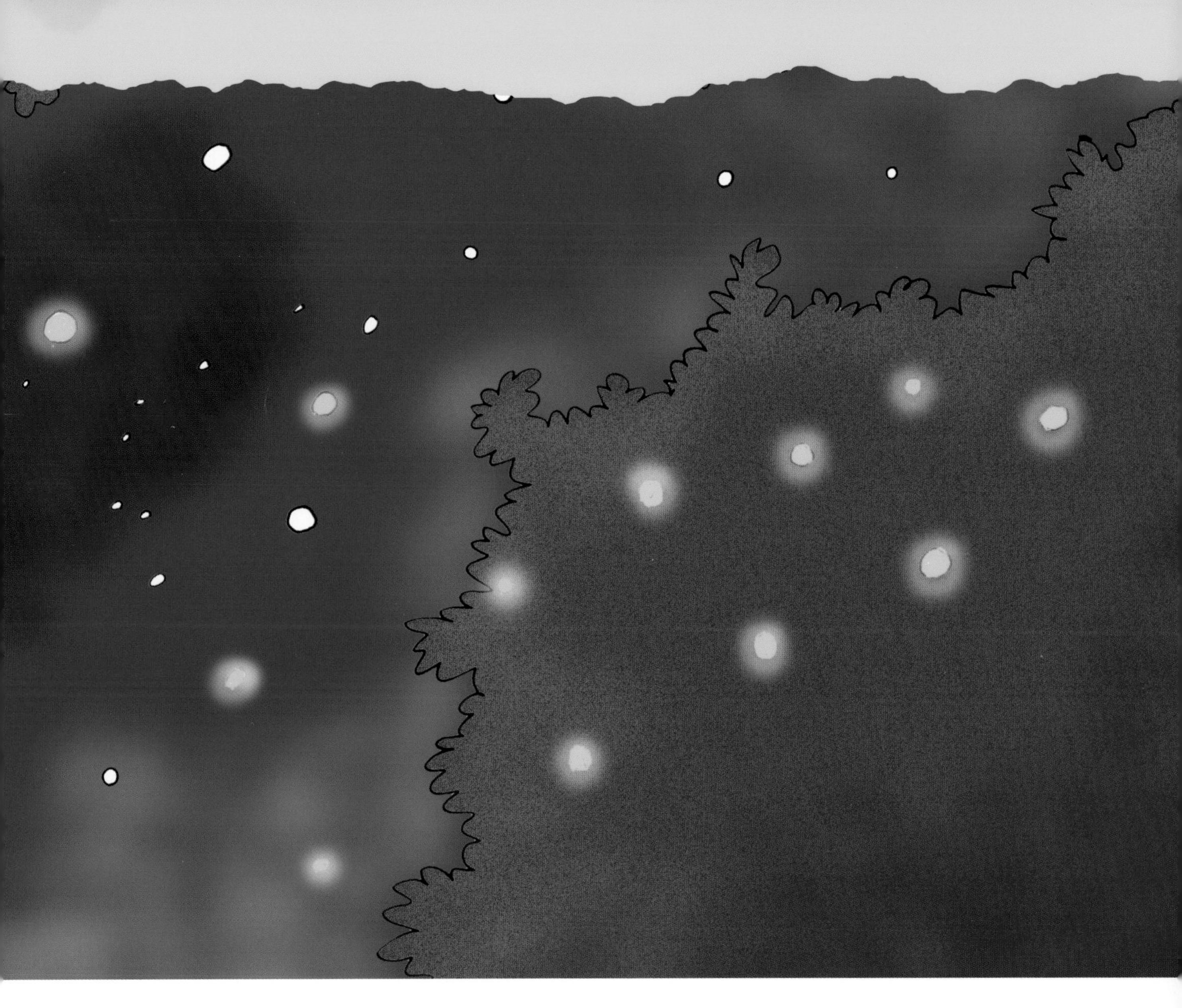

Caillou was too excited to sleep. He'd just spotted some small lights flickering in the air.

"Grandpa, what are those lights over there in the bushes?"
"Those aren't lights, Caillou. They're fireflies. Let's see if we can catch one."
Just then, a firefly landed right on Caillou's nose. Thrilled, he cupped his hands around it.

"Look, I caught one!"
"Good for you!" said Grandpa, smiling.
Then Caillou opened his hands and let the firefly go.

Caillou was stretched out in his sleeping bag. It was late, but he still couldn't get to sleep. Whoo! Whoo! Whoo! It was the hoot of an owl. Caillou opened his eyes and looked over at Grandpa, who was asleep beside him.

Caillou was getting scared, so he shook Grandpa to wake him up.
Right away, Grandpa guessed what was wrong. He knew just what to do!

The next morning, a ray of sunlight shone into the tent. Gilbert was curled up in a ball on Caillou's sleeping bag.
"Good morning, campers! Did you sleep well?" Mommy had come to wake them.

Gilbert got up and stretched. Caillou and Grandpa stuck their heads through the tent.
"What happened?" Mommy asked.
"There were strange sounds in the dark, so we decided to put up our tent inside the house," Grandpa explained.

Gilbert rubbed against Caillou. "I went camping with Grandpa!" Caillou announced proudly.
"Next time we go camping," said Grandpa, "we'll ask that owl to be quiet!"
Caillou hugged Gilbert and laughed happily.

Text adapted by Roger Harvey from the scenario of the CAILLOU animated film series produced by CINAR Corporation (© 1997 Caillou Productions Inc., a subsidiary of CINAR Corporation). All rights reserved.
Original scenario written by Caroline Maria
Illustrations taken from the television series CAILLOU.
Graphic design: Monique Dupras
Computer graphics: Les Studios de la Souris Mécanique

Canadian Cataloguing in Publication Data

Harvey, Roger, 1940 -
Caillou goes camping
(Backpack Collection)
Translation of: Caillou fait du camping.
For children aged 3 and up.
Co-published by Chouette Publishing (1987) Inc. and CINAR Corporation.

ISBN 2-89450-142-0

1. Camping – Juvenile literature. I. CINAR Corporation.
II. Title III. Series.

GV191.7.H3513 2000 j796.54 C99-941075-X

Legal deposit 2000

We gratefully acknowledge the financial support of BPIDP, SODEC, and the Canada Council for the Arts for our publishing activities.

Printed in Canada
10 9 8 7 6 5 4